For my best friend, Rafał

Published by Princeton Architectural Press
202 Warren Street
Hudson, New York 12534
www.papress.com

First published in France under the title *Mais où a filé Malo la musaraigne ?*
© 2018, hélium / Actes Sud, Paris, France.
Published by arrangement with Debbie Bibo Agency

ISBN 978-1-61689-875-5

This book was illustrated using watercolors.

For Princeton Architectural Press:
Editor: Parker Menzimer
Designer: Paula Baver

Special thanks to: Janet Behning, Abby Bussel, Jan Cigliano Hartman,
Susan Hershberg, Kristen Hewitt, Stephanie Holstein, Lia Hunt,
Valerie Kamen, Jennifer Lippert, Sara McKay, Wes Seeley, Rob Shaeffer,
Sara Stemen, Jessica Tackett, Marisa Tesoro, Paul Wagner, and Joseph Weston
of Princeton Architectural Press
—Kevin C. Lippert, publisher

Library of Congress Cataloging-in-Publication Data
available upon request

MALO
AND THE
MERRY-GO-
ROUND

Maria Dek

PRINCETON ARCHITECTURAL PRESS · NEW YORK

Poto was making pickles on his porch. Malo, his best friend, had promised to help him.

But one of them wasn't so eager to work on such a pretty day.

"I don't want to make pickles," Malo mumbled.
"Let's go chase beetles!"

"But you said you'd help me," Poto complained.
"And, besides, I have big news!"

Malo's ears perked up.

"There's a new merry-go-round
at the pond in the forest.
I saw it! It's gigantic.
After we make pickles, we'll go,"
Poto said. "What do you say?"

But there was no answer.

Malo had already sneaked past the porch on his way to find the merry-go-round.

Malo passed by a wild boar.
"Help me!" the boar groaned. "This tick is biting me,
but I can't reach it. Could you please get it off?"

Malo sighed.
Helping the boar
would take time, and
the merry-go-round
was waiting.
"I'm in a terrible rush,"
Malo said,
and he made a
dash for it.

At the foot of the hill, a gang of forest turtles
crossed Malo's path.

"Where are you going, Malo?"
"Can we come with you?"
"We could have so much fun playing together
 in the forest!"
"Please can we come? Please?" they squeaked.

"I don't have time. I'm going to Poto's to make pickles,"
 Malo lied before darting away.

Malo arrived at the forest.
He looked for the merry-go-round but
he couldn't see it through the thick trees.
Luckily, there was a cuckoo sitting high
in the branches.

"Where's the pond?" Malo called.
"Let me think," the cuckoo coo-cooed thoughtfully.
"Coo-coo could you hurry up?"
  Malo snapped, shuffling his feet impatiently.

  But the bird didn't know where the pond was.
  In a huff, Malo walked off.

Malo climbed onto a stump to get
a better look.

There it was! The merry-go-round!
Malo bounced happily up and down,
but then…

SWOOSH...!

...he slipped on a dung beetle's ball of dung.
The dung beetle was not happy.

Neither was Malo. His feet and fur were covered.
Furiously, he continued on his way.

When Malo finally reached the merry-go-round
he clambered into a seat.
But for some reason, he was no longer excited.
Perhaps it was because he was tired.
Or maybe it was the dung.
But then, maybe it was something else...

Suddenly, making pickles with Poto sounded fun.
"I wish Poto was here," Malo sighed.

Malo rushed back to
Poto's house, his heart
beating fast.

Poto was still on his porch
but he had finished making pickles.
He looked pretty sad.

Malo approached him sheepishly.
"I'm sorry," he said.

"I went to the merry-go-round,
but it was no fun without you.
And I fell in poop! I promise to
make pickles with you next time."

"You fell in poop?" Poto laughed.

"Yes. It was awful.
And I wasn't very nice to a boar.
I lied to the forest turtles.
I was rude to a cuckoo bird," Malo confessed.
"Will you help me make things right?"

"Of course," Poto said. "I'm your best friend!"

Malo and Poto found the boar.
"I'm sorry," Malo said.
And together they helped
the boar get rid of the tick.

Then they found the cuckoo.
Malo apologized for being rude

and gave her a delicious worm.

Next, they visited the dung beetle.
Malo apologized for smooshing his
ball of dung.

But Malo and Poto couldn't find
the forest turtles.

Finally, they found them at the
merry-go-round.

The turtles were still a bit hurt.

"I'm really sorry," Malo said.
"Do you still want to play?"

The turtles huddled together and
decided that Malo could spin them
on the merry-go-round.

Everyone took a seat, and Malo spun them round and round.

Their day of fun had just begun.